JUST FOR YOU

BY

MERCER MAYER

A GOLDEN BOOK • NEW YORK

Western Publishing Company, Inc.
Racine, Wisconsin 53404

ISBN 0-307-63542-7   d e f g h i j k l m

This morning I wanted
to make breakfast just for you...
but the eggs
were too slippery.

I wanted to wash the floor
just for you,
but the soap was too bubbly.

I wanted to put away the dishes
just for you,
but the floor was too wet.

I wanted to carry the groceries
just for you,
but the bag broke.

I ate my sandwich
just for you,
but not my crusts.

I wanted to take a nap
just for you,
but the bed was too bouncy.

I wanted to mow the lawn
just for you,
but I was too little.

I picked an apple
just for you,
but on the way home
I got hungry.

I wanted to set the table
just for you,
but the TV was too loud.

I wanted to
not splash in my bath
just for you...

...but there was a storm.

I wanted to do something very special,

just for you.

And I did it.